A Note to Parents and Caregivers:

Read-it! Readers are for children who are just starting on the amazing road to reading. These beautiful books support both the acquisition of reading skills and the love of books.

 The PURPLE LEVEL presents basic topics and objects using high frequency words and simple language patterns.

 The RED LEVEL presents familiar topics using common words and repeating sentence patterns.

 The BLUE LEVEL presents new ideas using a larger vocabulary and varied sentence structure.

 The YELLOW LEVEL presents more challenging ideas, a broad vocabulary, and wide variety in sentence structure.

 The GREEN LEVEL presents more complex ideas, an extended vocabulary range, and expanded language structures.

 The ORANGE LEVEL presents a wide range of ideas and concepts using challenging vocabulary and complex language structures.

When sharing a book with your child, read in short stretches, pausing often to talk about the pictures. Have your child turn the pages and point to the pictures and familiar words. And be sure to reread favorite stories or parts of stories.

There is no right or wrong way to share books with children. Find time to read with your child, and pass on the legacy of literacy.

Adria F. Klein, Ph.D.
Professor Emeritus
California State University
San Bernardino, California

For my GREAT-aunt Mutzie Meinhardt (Manderfeld)—J.K.

Editor: Christianne Jones
Designer: Hilary Wacholz
Page Production: Melissa Kes
Art Director: Nathan Gassman
The illustrations in this book were created with watercolor and pen.

Picture Window Books
151 Good Counsel Drive
P.O. Box 669
Mankato, MN 56002-0669
877-845-8392
www.picturewindowbooks.com

Printed in the United States of America.

Library of Congress Cataloging-in-Publication Data
Kalz, Jill.
Tuckerbean at Big Bone Bowl / by Jill Kalz ; illustrated by Benton Mahan.
p. cm. — (Read-it! readers)
ISBN 978-1-4048-4747-7 (library binding)
[1. Bowling—Fiction. 2. Dogs—Fiction.] I. Mahan, Ben, ill. II. Title.
PZ7.K12655Tucc 2008
[E]—dc22
                                    2008006312

Tuckerbean
at
Big Bone Bowl

by Jill Kalz
illustrated by Benton Mahan

Special thanks to our reading adviser:

Adria F. Klein, Ph.D.
Professor Emeritus, California State University
San Bernardino, California

PiCTURE WiNDOW BOOKS
Minneapolis, Minnesota

4

Tuckerbean's three favorite people in the world are Peni, Peni's mom, and Grandma Tootie.

Grandma Tootie lives far away. When she visits, the house fills with smiles and giggles.

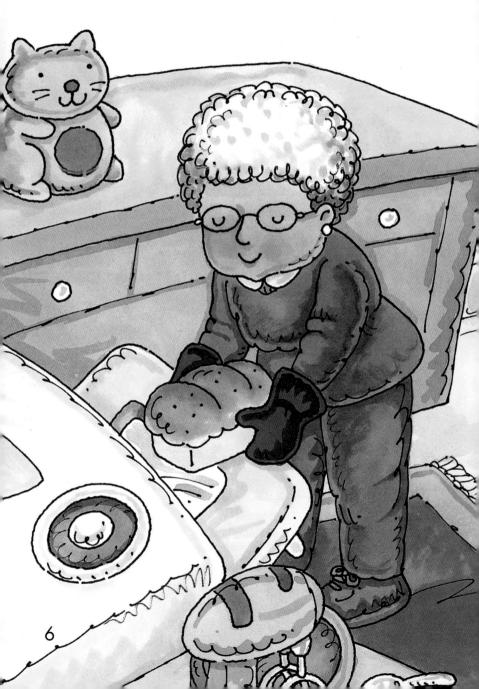

It smells like banana bread.

Peni shows Grandma Tootie her new red dress.
Grandma Tootie claps.

Tuckerbean shows her his new squeaky toy.
Grandma Tootie whistles.

After supper, Grandma Tootie sneaks out the back door. Tuckerbean sneaks out, too. They have a secret.

11

They love to go bowling!

13

When Tuckerbean knocks down all of the pins, Grandma Tootie yells, "Strike!"

When Grandma Tootie knocks down all of the pins, Tuckerbean does a flip.

17

Sometimes, they don't knock down any pins.

18

19

Grandma Tootie wins the last game. She shares a peanut butter cookie with Tuckerbean.

Back at home, Tuckerbean climbs into bed.

Grandma Tootie snores. They have happy dreams all night long.

More *Read-it!* Readers

Bright pictures and fun stories help you practice your reading skills. Look for more books at your level.

On the Web

FactHound offers a safe, fun way to find Web sites related to topics in this book. All of the sites on FactHound have been researched by our staff.

1. Visit *www.facthound.com*

2. Type in this special code:
   1404847472

3. Click on the FETCH IT button.

Your trusty FactHound will fetch the best sites for you!
A complete list of *Read-it!* Readers is available on our Web site:
www.picturewindowbooks.com

24